There Was an Old Lady Who Swallowed a Fly

A play based on a traditional poem

by Mark Carthew with Michael Rosen

Illustrated by Ann James

D0334176

Collins

Characters

Reader 1

Reader 2

Reader 3

Reader 4

Reader 5

Old Lady

Turn to page **13** for Sound and Stage Tips

There Was an Old Lady Who Swallowed a Fly

Reader 1: There was an old lady
who swallowed a fly.

Old Lady: MY! MY!

Reader 2: Poor old lady, she'll surely die.

Reader 3: There was an old lady
who swallowed a spider.

Old Lady: Whoops!

Reader 4: It went right down inside her.

Reader 5: She swallowed the spider to eat up the fly.

Old Lady: MY! MY!

All: Poor old lady, she'll surely die.

Reader 1: There was an old lady
who swallowed a bird.

Reader 2: How absurd! She swallowed a bird.

Reader 3: She swallowed the bird
to eat up the spider.

Old Lady: Whoops!

Reader 4: It went right down inside her.

Reader 5: She swallowed the spider to eat up the fly.

Old Lady: MY! MY!

All: Poor old lady,
she'll surely die.

Reader 1: There was an old lady
who swallowed a cat.

Reader 2: Fancy that! She swallowed a cat.

Reader 3: She swallowed the cat to eat up the bird.

Reader 4: How absurd! She swallowed a bird.

Reader 5: She swallowed the bird
to eat up the spider.

Old Lady: Whoops!

Reader 4: It went right down inside her.

Reader 3: She swallowed the spider to eat up the fly.

Old Lady: MY! MY!

All: Poor old lady, she'll surely die.

Reader 1:   There was an old lady
who swallowed a dog.

Reader 2:   The hog! To swallow a dog.

Reader 3:   She swallowed the dog to eat up the cat.

Reader 4:   Fancy that! She swallowed a cat.

Reader 5:   She swallowed the cat to eat up the bird.

Reader 4: How absurd! She swallowed a bird.

Reader 3: She swallowed the bird
to eat up the spider.

Old Lady: Whoops!

Reader 2: It went right down inside her.

Reader 1: She swallowed the spider to eat up the fly.

Old Lady: MY! MY!

All: Poor old lady, she'll surely die.

Reader 1:   There was an old lady
who swallowed a cow.

Reader 2:   How now! She swallowed a cow.

Reader 3:   She swallowed the cow to eat up the dog.

Reader 4:   The hog! To swallow a dog.

Reader 5: She swallowed the dog to eat up the cat.

Reader 4: Fancy that! She swallowed a cat.

Reader 3: She swallowed the cat to eat up the bird.

Reader 2: How absurd! She swallowed a bird.

Reader 1: She swallowed the bird
to eat up the spider.

Old Lady: Whoops!

Reader 2: It went right down inside her.

Reader 3: She swallowed the spider to eat up the fly.

Old Lady: MY! MY!

All: Poor old lady, she'll surely die.

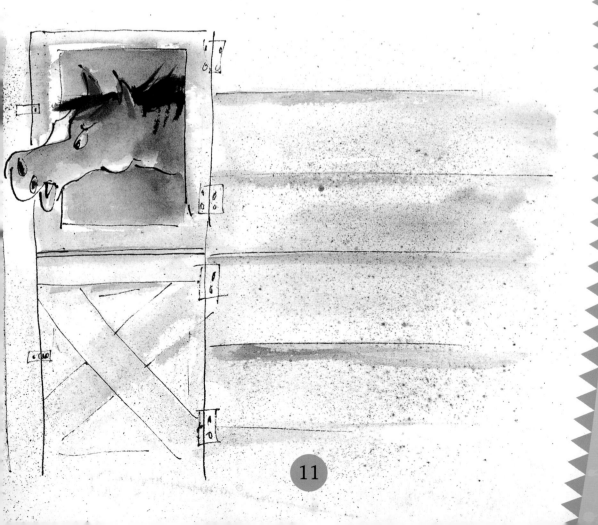

Reader 4: There was an old lady
who swallowed a horse.

All: Poor old lady …

Reader 5: She died of course.

Sound and Stage Tips

About This Play

This play is a story you can read with your friends in a group or act out in front of an audience. Before you start reading, choose a part or parts you would like to read or act.

There are six main parts in this play, so make sure you have readers for all the parts. You may also wish to have non-speaking, walk-on parts for the fly, spider, bird, cat, dog, cow and horse.

Reading the Play

It's a good idea to read the play through to yourself before you read it as part of a group. It is best to have your own book, as that will help you too. As you read the play through, think about each character and how they might look and sound. How are they behaving? What sort of voice might they have?

Rehearsing the Play

Rehearse the play a few times before you perform it for others. In *There Was an Old Lady Who Swallowed a Fly*, it is important for each reader to follow on smoothly from the previous reader. It is a good idea to practise this.

Remember you are an actor as well as a reader. Your facial expressions and the way you move your body will really help the play to come alive!

Using Your Voice

Remember to speak out clearly and be careful not to read too quickly!
Speak more slowly than you do when you're speaking to your friends.
Keep in mind that the audience is hearing your words for the first time.
It is important for each Reader to slow down and wait for the Old Lady
to say 'Whoops!' or 'My! My!'. Then all the Readers should say together,
'Poor old lady, she'll surely die!'.

Remember to look at the audience and at the other actors, making
sure everyone can hear what you are saying.

Creating Sound Effects (FX)

You might like to add the sounds of the various creatures just before
the Old Lady swallows them! For example, the 'Buzzz' of a fly or the
'Mooo' of a cow!

meow! moo! neigh!
psssss! woof! bzzzzz!
burp! tweet!

Sets and Props

Once you have read the play, make a list of the things you will need.
What you need most in this play is your voice! However, some chairs or
stools for the Readers may also be useful.

Costumes

This play can be performed with or without costumes. If you wish to dress up, you may find the following useful.

- Dress, shawl, glasses and headscarf for the Old Lady
- Simple animal costumes, such as wings for the fly, eight legs for the spider and a tail for the horse (if you decide to have parts for the animals)

cat

bird

dog

old lady

fly

cow

spider

horse

Have fun!

Ideas for guided reading

Learning objectives: read, prepare and present playscripts; take account of the grammar and punctuation when reading aloud; recognise the key differences between prose and playscript, e.g. by looking at dialogue, stage directions, layout of text in prose and playscripts; present events and characters through dialogue to engage the interest of an audience

Curriculum links: Music: The class orchestra – Exploring arrangements

Interest words: swallowed, surely, absurd, fancy

Resources: musical instruments, e.g. xylophone; large card for cue cards, marker pens

Casting: there are 6 equal speaking parts

Getting started

- Ask the children if they know this story already. Prompt them to discuss its usual form, i.e. a poem or song. Discuss how this version could be different and what the advantages and disadvantages might be.

- Look at the characters on p2. Discuss how this play can be made interesting when there are so many readers telling the story (e.g. the use of sound effects and a variety of voices).

- Look at pp3–5 and discuss the features of a playscript (the character name on left-hand side, dialogue rather than reported speech, etc).

- Ask the children to read p3 silently and consider how they would make their voices different for each part (e.g. pitch, volume and rhythm of speech).

- Ask the children to consider the importance of rhythm and phrasing. Give a bad example (i.e. reading without emphasising the rhymes) and ask the children how it could be improved.

Reading and responding

- Read pp6–12 silently, focusing on building up speed and fluency, in preparation for a group reading. Discuss how *My, my!* should be read, and the role of the exclamation marks in the play (for expression).

- Discuss the structure of this 'story' and how it builds up. Ask the group to plot the chain of events as the old lady swallows things.

- What is the message or purpose of this story?